This book belongs to

Lois

Barbie™
in
The Mystical Moonflower

Illustrations by Christian Musselman
Cover illustration by Lawrence Mann

EGMONT

EGMONT

We bring stories to life

This edition published in Great Britain 2008
by Egmont UK Limited
239 Kensington High Street, London W8 6SA

BARBIE and associated trademarks and trade dress are owned by,
and used under licence from, Mattel, Inc.
© 2008 Mattel, Inc.

1 3 5 7 9 10 8 6 4 2

Printed in China

Hello, I'm Marina the mermaid and I live in the Coral Kingdom. This is a story about what happened when a mysterious object arrived in our beautiful Blue Lagoon . . .

The Blue Lagoon was dark, deep and mysterious. In the rippling shallows all was calm, except for the soft sound of water lapping to and fro against the rim of a half-moon beach.

Deep down in the murky depths, behind a clump of waving weeds, came the muffled sounds of something stretching and growing . . .

Something put out its feelers, scattering sand and sending up a stream of silvery bubbles from the lagoon floor. It drifted upwards, pulling a trail of tendrils behind it . . .

It was an early midsummer's evening. Curly, the little seahorse, swam quickly to his friend Marina's side. "Something strange has happened," he told her. "Come and see!"

Marina and Curly swam up through the shimmering light to see a Mystical Thing floating on the surface of the water, glowing softly.

"What can it be?" Marina wondered. She blew on her conch to call the creatures of the Lagoon, who came to take a look.

"Oh, no!" the frightened little fish cried, "the Moon has fallen out of the sky. We will have to put it back before nightfall!"

Before Marina could tell the creatures that this could not be the Moon, they had gathered together and were pushing the Mystical Thing as hard as they could. The friends huffed and puffed, but it wouldn't budge.

"Stop! Stop!" Marina called to her friends. "This isn't the Moon, it has tendrils! Please don't push it, you might hurt it."

Curly swam back and forth, peering closely at the Mystical Thing then darting back to Marina, looking puzzled, before zipping back to take another peep.

Suddenly, his curly tail became tangled in the tendrils! Marina and her friends pulled together to free the scared little seahorse.

"I don't like that big Thing," Curly scowled, tugging at one long, wavy, pink tendril.

"Curly, I'm sure it didn't mean to tangle you up. Please don't pull its tendrils," warned Marina.

The friends tried to guess what the Thing could be.

"Perhaps it's a mean sea monster," moaned the mitten crab mournfully, clicking his claws.

"Perhaps it's an angry octopus," squealed Curly, spinning round and round on his tail.

"Perhaps it's a grumpy Giant Clam, too cowardly to show his face," wondered the lonely lobster. "Come out, come out!"

The lobster began to tap the object with his claws to see if it would open.

"Please, leave it be!" Marina pleaded. "We have to look after this Thing, whatever it might be."

Suddenly Marina had an idea.

"We should ask the Medusa what it is," the clever mermaid said. "She is such a wise jellyfish. She will surely know. Come, Curly, let us bring the magic seaweed that will make the Medusa talk to us."

Marina and Curly set off on their journey to the Medusa's grotto . . . but the Mystical Thing followed them!

"Help! Help!" Curly squealed. "It's chasing us!"

"It won't hurt us," Marina reassured the little seahorse, but Curly hid behind a rock and wouldn't come out until the Thing was out of sight.

Marina swam to the Medusa's grotto alone. The Medusa floated out to greet the mermaid, who showed her the Mystical Thing.

"This wonderful, Mystical Thing has appeared in our Blue Lagoon," Marina explained, "and we don't know what it is. Do you know, please, wise Medusa?"

The Medusa peered up at the Mystical Thing. "Why, Marina, this is a Mystical Moonflower, a thing of beauty, one of Nature's gifts! It blooms when the Moon is as blue as the sky at noon."

"Why did it follow us to your grotto?" Marina wondered as she peered up at the pretty, shimmering flower.

"It has come to deliver a message," the wise Medusa told the mermaid. "You must return to the Lagoon and await the message there."

So Marina began the journey back to the Lagoon, coaxing Curly out from the rocks on her way.

At the Blue Lagoon, Marina's marine friends gathered around her, staring in fear at the Mystical Moonflower, begging for an explanation.

But before Marina could comfort her friends and tell them that the Moonflower meant no harm, a full, blue Moon rose, and bathed the Blue Lagoon in her milky rays.

Marina and her Blue Lagoon companions watched open-mouthed as the giant pod slowly unfurled, one silvery segment after another, and out stepped a beautiful fairy. The sea creatures forgot their fears and were fascinated by the flower.

The fairy gently cast pearly seeds into the water, and more Moonflowers bloomed all around, turning the Lagoon into a floating meadow!

"I am the Moon Maiden," the fairy declared, "and I come to deliver a message to you, Marina!"

The Moon Maiden spoke in a silvery voice that captivated everyone around her. "Marina, you have protected our Mystical Moonflower and cared for the sea's creatures. Mother Moon wishes to reward you. As a symbol of her blessing, the sea will flourish with life and the tides will continue to rise and fall as surely as the Moon waxes and wanes."

Sure enough, thousands of brightly coloured fish swam from far and wide to paint the Lagoon with rainbow shades.

"Our Lagoon is so beautiful and full of life!" Marina exclaimed. "We must celebrate!" Marina's fishtail friends gurgled in agreement. "We must have a party – a Blue Moon Ball!"

That mystical evening, Marina and her friends crowned the Moon Maiden their Moonflower Princess to the brassy blare of the trumpetfish. She was towed along on a Moonflower barge by sailfish gently flapping their fins.

At daybreak, as the Moon dipped into the water, Marina and the mermaids bathed in its soft beams. They sang sweet songs to the waves on the slumbering shore. Marina invited the Moon Maiden to join in.

"Thank you, Marina, you are very kind," the Moon Maiden smiled, "but I must return to Mother Moon!"

Marina and her friends waved as the Maiden flew on silvery wings home to the Moon. The Mystical Moonflower's giant petals curled up, and it drifted to its resting place on the seabed.

Here it would hide, until the next blue moonrise.

Magical titles in this series:

Look out for more enchanting tales to add to your collection!